When Making New Friends

Davidna A. Palmer

The Reading Glass Books
(888) 420-3050
www.readingglassbooks.com
fulfillment@readingglassbooks.com

When Making New Friends

"Hi, boys and girls! My name is Anna Apple. Do you want to go on an adventure with me? Great! Let's go to the park."

"Hi, I'm Anna Apple. What's your name?"
"I'm Bo Banana."
"Nice to meet you, Bo Banana!"

"WHEE-HEE!"
"Who's that?" asked Bo Banana.
"I don't know," replied Anna Apple. "Sounds like it's coming from the slide. Let's go make friends!"

"Hi! I'm Anna Apple, and this is my friend Bo Banana. What are your names?"
"Well, I'm Carol Carrot, and this is my friend Tommy Tomato."

"Do you all want to play a game?" asked Bo Banana.
"Sure!"
"Okay, fruits against vegetables."

"That wouldn't be fair," said Tommy Tomato. "That would leave Carol Carrot all alone."

"I am confused," said Bo Banana. "You are a vegetable, so you could be on her team."

"I'm not a vegetable. I'm a fruit!"
"Wait a minute! Fruits are sweet," said Bo Banana.

"Not all of us," replied Tommy Tomato.

"My parents say a fruit is anything with seeds, and guess what! I have seeds," said Tommy Tomato.

"I still don't believe you are a fruit," said Bo Banana.

Just as they were talking, Jack the farmer was walking by with his dog, Sparky.

"Let's go ask him!" said Carol Carrot.

They all ran to Jack the farmer.

"Am I a fruit or a vegetable?" asked Tommy Tomato.

"Why, you are a handsome little fruit, Tommy!"
"I told you! Thanks, Farmer Jack."
"You're welcome. I'm glad I could help."

They all started on their way back to the park.

Bo Banana said, "I'm sorry I didn't believe you, Tommy Tomato. I really did not know. Please forgive me."

"I forgive you, Bo Banana. Let's all remember, you can't really know someone just by looking at them from the outside. You have to ask questions, become friends, and then you find out who they are on the inside."

“Yeah, the inside is what matters! Now can we all go play?” asked Anna Apple.

They all replied with a loud, “Yes!”

Lessons Learned

1. Did Bo Banana believe that Tommy Tomato was a fruit? Why or why not?

2. What really matters?

3. How do you find out what's on the inside?

4. Name 3 fruits that you love.

5. Name 3 vegetables that you love.

____

____

____

6. Circle the fruits:

green beans potato grape

squash celery broccoli

About the Author

As a person who can appreciate the lessons of her past, Davidna realizes that she has had many teachers along the way. These teachers ranged in age, socioeconomic status, and ethnic background. By observing them, Davidna has learned what "to do" and what "not to do" in various aspects of her life. As a proud wife and mother, Davidna has come to accept that not only is she still learning and observing but that she, too, is a teacher. She desires that the mark she leaves on not just the world, but on each and every heart she encounters be one of peace, encouragement, and most importantly, love.